# THE HIDDEN

ONE DAY, LONG LONG AGO, A WOMAN CAME WALKING DEJECTEDLY DOWN THE ROAD THAT LED AWAY FROM THE CITY OF MITHILA. HER STEPS WERE SLOW AND HER FEET DRAGGED.

SHE WORE THE GARB OF A MAID BUT SEEMED TO BE OF NOBLE BIRTH.

I CANNOT WALK A STEP FARTHER. WHAT SHALL I DO? PERHAPS THAT CARTER WILL...

HOW FAR ARE YOU GOING, SIR? CAN YOU TAKE ME TO KALACHAMPA?

SHE LOOKS TIRED AND MISERABLE, POOR THING.

I'LL TAKE YOU THERE. PLEASE GET INTO MY CART.

YOU ARE VERY KIND, SIR! I...I DON'T KNOW HOW TO THANK YOU.

I CANNOT BELIEVE MY GOOD LUCK. THE GODS ARE WITH ME, TO BE SURE!

AS THE CART JOGGED ALONG, THE EXHAUSTED WOMAN FELL ASLEEP.

WHEN SHE WOKE UP IT WAS EVENING.

WHICH CITY IS THIS?

WHY, IT'S THE CITY OF KALACHAMPA! WE HAVE ARRIVED.

HE BROUGHT HIS CART TO A HALT AT THE SOUTHERN GATE OF THE CITY.

IT WILL BE EASIER FOR YOU TO ENTER THE CITY FROM HERE.

I AM GRATEFUL TO YOU FOR BRINGING ME HERE, KIND SIR.

AFTER ALIGHTING FROM THE CART...

...SHE WALKED INTO THE CITY.

I CAME HERE BECAUSE THIS WAS THE ONLY CITY I'D HEARD OF. WHERE SHALL I GO NOW?

A LITTLE LATER, A TEACHER CAME BY WITH HIS PUPILS.

SURPRISED TO SEE A WOMAN SITTING THERE ALONE, HE WALKED UP TO HER.

WHO ARE YOU? YOU SEEM TO BE IN DISTRESS.

I...I AM...

THE BRAHMANA TOOK HER TO HIS WIFE.

MY SISTER HAS COME TO LIVE WITH US. SHE'S GOING TO HAVE A BABY. PLEASE TAKE CARE OF HER.

WELCOME HOME, SISTER. I AM SO GLAD YOU HAVE COME TO US.

THE BRAHMANA AND HIS WIFE LOOKED AFTER HER WITH LOVE AND CARE. AFTER A FEW DAYS, A SON WAS BORN TO HER.

WHAT SHALL WE CALL HIM, BROTHER?

WE'LL CALL HIM MAHAJANAKA.

THE QUEEN AND HER SON STAYED ON IN THE HOUSE OF THE KIND BRAHMANA AND HIS WIFE.

HOW HAPPY I AM THAT WE ARE STILL ALIVE AND WELL.

WHEN MAHAJANAKA GREW A LITTLE OLDER, HE MADE FRIENDS WITH THE BOYS IN THE NEIGHBOURHOOD.

COME ON, MAHAJANAKA. WE ARE WAITING FOR YOU.

I'M COMING!

BUT THEY OFTEN QUARRELLED TOO. AND, THEN, MAHAJANAKA WHO WAS THE STRONGEST OF THEM ALL, WOULD BEAT UP THE OTHERS. ONE DAY, AFTER SUCH A QUARREL —

I'LL GO AND TELL MY FATHER!

I'LL ALSO GO AND TELL MY...

WHO? WHO WOULD YOU TELL?

YOU HAVE NO FATHER!

HE HAS NO FATHER!

HA! HA!

HE HAS NO FATHER!

MAHAJANAKA RAN TO HIS MOTHER.

MOTHER, THEY SAY I HAVE NO FATHER. THEY SAY...

OH, MOTHER! WHO IS MY FATHER?

I'LL TELL YOU, SON. BUT DON'T CRY. PLEASE DON'T... THAT'S A GOOD BOY!

NOW TELL ME.

HOW CAN I, SON? OUR ENEMIES SHOULDN'T KNOW THAT WE ARE ALIVE! OH, WHAT SHALL I DO?

WHY ARE YOU SILENT, MOTHER? TELL ME! TELL ME THE TRUTH!

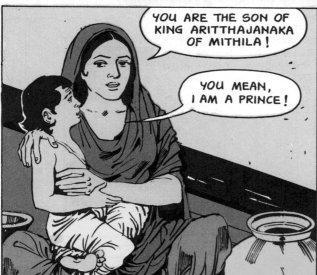

YOU ARE THE SON OF KING ARITTHAJANAKA OF MITHILA!

YOU MEAN, I AM A PRINCE!

"YES, YOU ARE A PRINCE. A FEW DAYS BEFORE YOU WERE BORN, YOUR FATHER HAD TO LEAVE TO DO BATTLE WITH HIS ENEMY, POLJANAKA."

IF ANYTHING SHOULD HAPPEN TO ME, YOU MUST PROTECT YOURSELF AND SAVE OUR CHILD.

"I WAITED ANXIOUSLY FOR NEWS OF THE BATTLE. THEN TOWARDS MIDDAY, A MESSENGER RUSHED IN."

WE HAVE LOST ...OUR KING IS NO MORE! POLJANAKA AND HIS MEN WILL BE HERE ANY MOMENT.

THE ENEMY WILL SOON BE HERE!

LET'S SAVE OURSELVES WHILE WE CAN.

MY LADY, I...I...

DO YOU WANT TO LEAVE TOO? I UNDERSTAND. YOU MAY GO.

MY WHOLE WORLD IS CRUMBLING AROUND ME. LIFE HAS NO MEANING ANY MORE. BUT I MUST STAY ALIVE FOR THE SAKE OF OUR CHILD.

"I TIED TOGETHER SOME GOLD COINS AND JEWELS AND PUT THE BUNDLE IN AN OLD BASKET."

"AFTER THAT I CAST OFF MY ROYAL CLOTHES, DISGUISED MYSELF AS A MAID AND LEFT THE PALACE WITH THE BASKET.

"A CARTER BROUGHT ME HERE TO KALACHAMPA."

IF IT WERE NOT FOR OUR HOST AND HIS WIFE, I DON'T KNOW WHAT WOULD HAVE HAPPENED TO ME ... AND LATER YOU.

EVEN NOW I AM AFRAID OF OUR ENEMIES. NOBODY SHOULD KNOW WHO WE ARE.

DON'T WORRY, MOTHER. NO ONE WILL. I PROMISE.

SOON AFTER THAT, HE STARTED STUDYING UNDER THE BRAHMANA.

I MUST WORK HARD. ONE DAY I WILL RULE OVER MITHILA.

9

YEARS PASSED. MAHAJANAKA GREW UP TO BE A HANDSOME AND LEARNED MAN. ONE DAY —

MOTHER, DO YOU HAVE ANY MONEY WITH YOU?

I DID NOT COME AWAY FROM MITHILA, EMPTY-HANDED. BUT WHY DO YOU ASK, MY SON?

I WISH TO GO TO MITHILA TO CLAIM MY THRONE.

MY SON, I HAVE BEEN WAITING ALL THESE YEARS FOR THIS DAY!

I HAVE A FEW GOLD COINS AND ORNAMENTS. THEY ARE ALL YOURS.

NO, MOTHER, NOT ALL. I SHALL TAKE HALF. THE REST YOU MUST KEEP.

WITH MY HALF I SHALL BUY SOME MERCHANDISE, CARRY ON TRADE OVERSEAS AND EARN THE MONEY I'LL NEED, TO RAISE AN ARMY.

SOON THE DAY OF DEPARTURE DAWNED.

MOTHER, BLESS ME! AND DON'T WORRY.

MAY GOD BE WITH YOU, MY SON.

AS THE SHIP SET SAIL —

I WONDER IF POLJANAKA IS STILL ALIVE. WILL I HAVE TO FIGHT HIM OR HIS SON? I WONDER WHAT AWAITS ME AT MITHILA.

POLJANAKA WAS ALIVE BUT SERIOUSLY ILL AND HE HAD NO SON.

HIS MINISTERS WERE WORRIED ABOUT THE FUTURE OF THE KINGDOM.

WHY DON'T WE ASK THE KING TO APPOINT A SUCCESSOR?

SO THEY WENT TO THE KING.

I HAVE GIVEN THE MATTER DEEP THOUGHT AND MADE MY DECISION. THE MAN MY DAUGHTER CHOOSES FOR A HUSBAND, SHALL BE THE KING.

YOUR MAJESTY, PRINCESS SHIVALI WILL CHOOSE A GOOD MAN BUT HOW CAN WE BE SURE THAT HE WILL MAKE A GOOD KING?

I HAVE THOUGHT ABOUT THAT TOO. HER SUITOR WILL HAVE TO PERFORM THREE TASKS TO PROVE HIS INTELLIGENCE, STRENGTH AND WISDOM.

FIRST, HE MUST POINT OUT THE HEAD OF THE PRINCESS' SQUARE BED. THEN HE MUST STRING A BOW WHICH WOULD ORDINARILY REQUIRE THE STRENGTH OF A THOUSAND MEN.

LASTLY, WITH THE HELP OF SIXTEEN CLUES, HE WILL HAVE TO FIND THE SIXTEEN POTS OF GOLD I'VE HIDDEN IN AND AROUND THE PALACE.

YOU MUST LET THE PRINCESS MARRY HIM, ONLY IF HE SUCCEEDS IN PERFORMING ALL THE TASKS.

A FEW DAYS LATER THE KING DIED.

SOON THE GENERAL STOOD BEFORE HER.

I AM AT YOUR SERVICE, PRINCESS.

WHAT CAN YOU DO FOR ME?

OH! ANYTHING! YOUR WORD IS MY COMMAND!

AH! IS THAT SO?

YES... I'LL STRIVE TO SERVE YOU IN EVERY WAY — EVEN PRESS YOUR FEET OR FETCH YOUR SLIPPERS!

I COULD NEVER RESPECT THIS SERVILE CREATURE!

HOW CAN YOU BE SO MEEK! HAVE YOU NO SELF-RESPECT? YOU MAY GO NOW, GENERAL!

WHEN THE GENERAL RETURNED TO THE MINISTERS —

WHAT HAPPENED? YOU LOOK CREST-FALLEN!

THAT GIRL IS HARD TO PLEASE!

14

PERHAPS THE TREASURER MIGHT SUCCEED WHERE THE GENERAL FAILED.

YES. HE IS WISE... AND HANDSOME.

SO THE TREASURER WAS SENT TO MEET THE PRINCESS. BUT HE TOO FAILED. SO DID ALL THE OTHERS WHO TRIED TO WOO HER.

MEANWHILE ON BOARD MAHAJANAKA'S SHIP —

THE SEA HAS SUDDENLY BECOME ROUGH. IT LOOKS AS IF IT'S GOING TO RAIN!

SOON, A STORM BROKE. WAVE AFTER MIGHTY WAVE LASHED AT THE SHIP.

I MUST REMAIN CALM! I MUST NOT PANIC.

HE MOVED NEARER THE MAST AND HELD ON TO IT WITH ALL HIS STRENGTH.

I HAVE A MISSION TO ACCOMPLISH. I MUST NOT LET DEATH ROB ME OF THE CHANCE TO REGAIN THE THRONE OF MITHILA.

AS THE SHIP SANK UNDER THE ONSLAUGHT OF THE WAVES, MAHAJANAKA TIGHTENED HIS GRIP ON THE MAST.

I WON'T GIVE UP! I WILL SURVIVE THIS ORDEAL. I MUST.

A FEW DAYS LATER, MAHA-JANAKA WAS WASHED ASHORE. WHEN HE OPENED HIS EYES —

WHERE AM I? WHAT AN EFFORT IT IS TO MOVE! BUT I MUST MUSTER ALL MY STRENGTH AND FIND MY WAY TO THE CITY.

LATER, IN A GARDEN OUTSIDE THE EASTERN GATE OF THE CITY, HE OVERHEARD TWO MEN TALKING.

...AND SO MITHILA IS STILL WITHOUT A KING!

WHAT'S THIS I HEAR!

I AM IN MITHILA! AND MITHILA IS WITHOUT A KING!

BUT I HAVE NEITHER WEAPONS NOR MONEY. I MUST MOVE CAUTIOUSLY. I MUST LIE DOWN AND GET SOME REST BEFORE I MAKE ANY PLANS.

AT THE PALACE, MEANWHILE —

NOT A SINGLE MAN IN THE KINGDOM HAS BEEN ABLE TO PLEASE THE PRINCESS.

FOR HOW LONG CAN THE KINGDOM REMAIN WITHOUT A KING?

PERHAPS, THE ROYAL PRIEST CAN HELP US.

WHEN THEY CONSULTED THE ROYAL PRIEST —

SEND OUT THE SACRED CHARIOT. IT WILL LEAD US TO THE RIGHT MAN.

THE NEWS OF THE CHARIOT BEING SENT OUT SPREAD LIKE WILDFIRE. EXCITED CITIZENS THRONGED THE STREETS.

THAT WAS THE BEST DECISION OUR MINISTERS COULD HAVE TAKEN.

I HAVE HEARD THAT THE CHARIOT HAS NEVER FAILED US IN THE PAST. IT WILL NOT FAIL US NOW.

AT THE AUSPICIOUS HOUR THE ROYAL PRIEST STOOD BEFORE THE CHARIOT.

LEAD US TO HIM WHO WILL PLEASE SHIVALI AND WHO IS FIT TO RULE A KINGDOM.

THE ROYAL PRIEST WITH THE MINISTERS WALKED BEHIND THE CHARIOT AS IT ROLLED PAST THE HOUSES OF THE GENERAL, THE TREASURER, AND ALL THE OTHER SUITORS.

SUDDENLY THE HORSES BROKE INTO A GALLOP.

DON'T TRY TO SLOW THEM DOWN. WE'LL KEEP PACE WITH THEM.

THE CHARIOT SPED ON TOWARDS THE EASTERN GATE OF THE CITY...

...AND THEN ENTERING THE GARDEN...

...CAME TO A HALT NEAR THE SPOT WHERE MAHAJANAKA LAY SLEEPING.

THE CHARIOT HAS NEVER FAILED US... BUT... HE'S A TOTAL STRANGER.

I HAVE AN IDEA. LET THE DRUMS BE BEATEN AND THE HORNS BE BLOWN. LET THERE BE A DEAFENING UPROAR.

HOW HE WAKES UP, WHAT HE DOES AND SAYS, WILL TELL US MUCH ABOUT HIM. HE'S STIRRING!

THE NOISE AROUND HIM AWOKE MAHAJANAKA.

WHAT A TERRIBLE DIN! WHY ARE ALL THESE PEOPLE HERE? HM.M.M. I'LL KNOW SOONER OR LATER.

WHEN THE DIN AWOKE HIM THERE WAS NO SIGN OF PANIC IN HIS EYES. THEN HE WENT BACK TO SLEEP WITHOUT BETRAYING THE SLIGHTEST CURIOSITY. HE EXPECTS AN EXPLANATION FROM US AND IS CONFIDENT OF GETTING IT. HE IS BRAVE, WISE AND NOBLE.

THE PRIEST CAME FORWARD.

RISE, O NOBLE ONE. THE KINGDOM AWAITS YOU!

WHEN MAHAJANAKA SAT UP, THE PRIEST EXPLAINED ALL TO HIM.

ARE YOU WILLING TO WOO OUR PRINCESS AND ATTEMPT THE TASKS?

I AM. LET'S GO TO THE PALACE.

LED BY MAHAJANAKA WHO WAS SEATED IN THE CHARIOT, THE PROCESSION WENDED ITS WAY TO THE PALACE.

LONG LIVE THE KING!

WHEN PRINCESS SHIVALI WAS TOLD ABOUT MAHAJANAKA —

A TOTAL STRANGER? THE CHARIOT MAY HAVE FOUND HIM TO BE THE RIGHT MAN. BUT WILL I? ASK HIM TO SEE ME AT ONCE.

SHIVALI'S MAID DID AS SHE WAS TOLD.

THE PRINCESS WANTS TO SEE YOU.

BUT MAHAJANAKA DID NOT MOVE. SOON ANOTHER MAID CAME IN.

THE PRINCESS IS WAITING FOR YOU IN HER CHAMBER.

ONLY WHEN A THIRD MAID BROUGHT THE SAME MESSAGE DID HE RESPOND.

TELL HER I'LL COME IN A MOMENT. ONE OF YOU STAY WITH ME AND SHOW ME THE WAY.

HE TOOK HIS OWN TIME TO GET UP AND WALKED SLOWLY, REGALLY TOWARDS THE PRINCESS' ROOM.

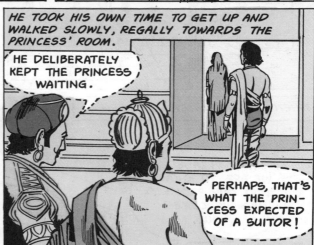

HE DELIBERATELY KEPT THE PRINCESS WAITING.

PERHAPS, THAT'S WHAT THE PRINCESS EXPECTED OF A SUITOR!

AS MAHAJANAKA WALKED AT A LEISURELY PACE UP THE STAIRS LEADING TO SHIVALI'S ROOM —

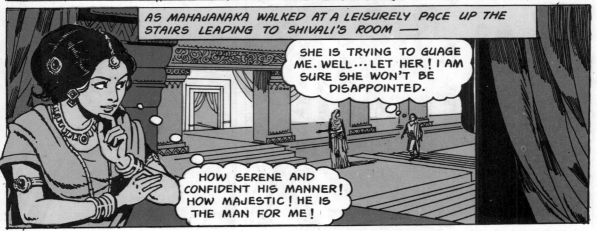

SHE IS TRYING TO GUAGE ME. WELL... LET HER! I AM SURE SHE WON'T BE DISAPPOINTED.

HOW SERENE AND CONFIDENT HIS MANNER! HOW MAJESTIC! HE IS THE MAN FOR ME!

SHE CAME OUT TO GREET HIM.

WELCOME, MY LORD!

LITTLE DID I DREAM THAT TO REGAIN MITHILA, I WOULD HAVE TO WIN THE RESPECT OF A PRINCESS AND NOT A BATTLE!

WON'T YOU COME IN? I'LL SEND FOR THE MINISTERS.

WHEN THE MINISTERS CAME —

HOW PLEASED WE ARE TO KNOW THAT OUR PRINCESS HAS WELCOMED YOU.

THE CHARIOT WAS RIGHT AS USUAL.

NOW FOR THE TASKS. FIRST YOU WILL HAVE TO FIND THE HEAD OF A SQUARE BED.

IS THAT ALL?

WHEN THEY WENT INSIDE —

HE SAT DOWN ON THE BED AND HELD OUT A PIN.

SOMETHING TELLS ME THAT HE'S GOING TO SUCCEED. AND I HOPE WITH ALL MY HEART THAT HE DOES.

THAT — THE PLACE WHERE SHIVALI WOULD NATURALLY PRESERVE HER PINS WHEN SHE REMOVES THEM — IS THE HEAD OF THE BED.

IT IS. HE IS RIGHT.

I HOPE THE NEXT TASK IS A MORE CHALLENGING ONE.

YOU'LL HAVE TO STRING THE GREAT BOW.

THEY WENT TO THE ARMOURY. THERE MAHAJANAKA WAS SHOWN THE BOW. HE LIFTED IT UP WITH EASE.

24

HE'S STRUNG IT! IT'S INCREDIBLE!

WELL DONE, MY LORD!

AND NOW?

THE LAST TEST. YOU HAVE TO FIND THE SIXTEEN POTS OF GOLD HIDDEN IN AND AROUND THE PALACE.

ARE THERE ANY CLUES?

YES, THERE ARE. YOU WILL FIND THE FIRST POT...

...WHERE THE SUN RISES; AND THE SECOND WHERE THE SUN SETS. THE THIRD...

THE MINISTER GAVE HIM THE REST OF THE CLUES. THEN —

FOR THIS TASK, I'LL NEED SOME TIME. BUT I'M SURE I'LL FIND ALL SIXTEEN POTS.

WE SINCERELY HOPE YOU DO.

THAT NIGHT MAHAJANAKA THOUGHT VERY HARD.

WHERE THE SUN RISES ...AND WHERE IT SETS..HMM ...THESE CAN'T SIMPLY BE EAST AND WEST. WHAT COULD IT BE...? SUN...

...SUN...SUN... THAT'S IT! THE SUN ALSO SYMBOLIZES LIGHT — THE LIGHT OF KNOWLEDGE AND TRUTH. NOW I KNOW!

THE NEXT MORNING WHEN THE MINISTERS ASSEMBLED IN THE HALL —

I'LL TRY TO FIND THE POTS TODAY. BUT, FIRST, I'D LIKE TO KNOW JUST ONE THING.

DID YOUR KING HONOUR ASCETICS AND SCHOLARS?

OH YES, HE DID! HE ALWAYS WORSHIPPED THEM LIKE GODS.

WHERE DID HE RECEIVE THEM WHEN THEY CAME?

COME WITH US, AND WE'LL SHOW YOU THE PLACE.

THE MINISTERS TOOK HIM OUTSIDE THE PALACE.

THIS IS WHERE THE KING RECEIVED ASCETICS AND SCHOLARS.

HAVE THIS PLACE DUG UP AND YOU WILL FIND THE FIRST POT.

THE PLACE WAS DUG UP. SOON —

LOOK! A HUGE POT!

REALLY? PULL IT UP QUICKLY.

THE POT WAS LIFTED UP AND OPENED.

GOLD! AND THERE ARE FIFTEEN MORE LIKE THIS.

NOW WHERE DID HE SEE THEM OFF?

THEY TOOK HIM TO THE SPOT.

THE KING ALWAYS ACCOMPANIED THEM UP TO THIS POINT. THIS IS WHERE HE SAW THEM OFF.

HMM! HAVE THIS PLACE DUG UP AND YOU'LL FIND THE SECOND POT.

AND TRUE ENOUGH THEY DID.

HOW DID YOU KNOW THAT THESE WERE THE SPOTS, MY LORD?

THE SUN MENTIONED BY THE KING IS NOT THE SUN WE KNOW. HE MEANT THE SUN OF KNOWLEDGE WITH WHICH SCHOLARS SHINE.

AFTER THIS MAHAJANAKA DECIPHERED THE REMAINING CLUES ONE AFTER THE OTHER AND ALL THE SIXTEEN POTS WERE FOUND.

YOU HAVE PROVED YOURSELF ON EVERY SCORE, MY LORD. YOU MUST NOW MARRY THE PRINCESS, AND MAKE US HAPPY.

THAT WILL HAVE TO WAIT FOR A WHILE.

FIRST, I WANT MY MOTHER AND MY UNCLE TO BE BROUGHT HERE FROM KALACHAMPA. PLEASE SEND SOMEONE TO FETCH THEM.

IT SHALL BE DONE AT ONCE.

AFTER A FEW WEEKS THE BRAHMANA ARRIVED WITH MAHAJANAKA'S MOTHER.

I AM SO HAPPY, SON. YOU HAVE DONE IT!

MOTHER!

MAHAJANAKA TURNED TO SHIVALI —

SHIVALI, MOTHER HAS COME HOME TODAY. SHE WAS THE QUEEN OF MITHILA ONCE.

WELCOME, MOTHER.

HE IS THE SON OF A KING! NO WONDER!

LATER, MAHAJANAKA AND SHIVALI WERE MARRIED.

WHAT A WELL-MATCHED COUPLE! HAD I NOT RUN AWAY FROM HERE WHEN MY LORD DIED, I WOULDN'T HAVE SEEN THIS DAY.

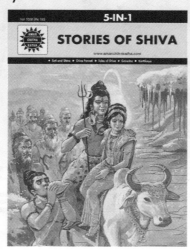

# SUBSCRIBE NOW!

**Pay only ₹~~1080~~ 800!**

**25% OFF**

## A twelve month subscription to TINKLE and TINKLE DIGEST

### YOUR DETAILS*

Student's Name _____

Parent's Name _____

Date of Birth: _____ (DD MM YYYY)

Address: _____

_____

_____

City: _____ PIN: _____

State: _____

School: _____

Class: _____

Email (Student): _____

Email (Parent): _____

Tel of Parent: (R): _____

Mobile: _____

_____

Parent's Signature: _____

*All the above fields are mandatory for the subscription to get activated.

### PAYMENT OPTIONS

☐ **Credit Card**
Card Type: Visa ☐ MasterCard ☐
Please charge ₹800 to my Credit Card Number
below: ☐☐☐☐ ☐☐☐☐ ☐☐☐☐ ☐☐☐☐
Expiry Date: ☐☐/☐☐

Cardmember's Signature:

☐ **CHEQUE / DD**
Enclosed please find cheque / DD no. ☐☐☐☐☐☐ drawn
favour of "ACK Media Direct Pvt. Ltd."
on (bank) _____
for the amount _____, dated ☐☐/☐☐/☐☐☐☐ an
send it to: **IBH magazine Service, Arch no.30, Below
Mahalaxmi Bridge, Near Racecourse, Mahalaxmi,
Mumbai 400034**

☐ **Pay by VPP**
Please pay the ₹800 to the postman on the delivery
of 1st issue. (Additional charges ₹30 apply)

☐ **Online subscription**
Visit www.amarchitrakatha.com

For any queries or further information please
write to us ACK Media Direct Pvt. Ltd.,
Krishna House, 3rd Floor, Raghuvanshi Mills Compund,
Sènapati Bapat Marg, Lower Parel, Mumbai 400 013.
Tel: 022-40 49 74 36
or send us an Email at customercare@ack-media.com